Limerick County Library

30012 00649492 5

D0718136

WITHDRAWN FROM STOCK

DRAWN FROM STOCK

A TEMPLAR BOOK

First published in the UK in 2008 by Templar Publishing,
an imprint of The Templar Company plc,
The Granary, North Street, Dorking, Surrey, RH4 1DN, UK

Illustration copyright © 2008 by Jonathan Lambert
Text and design copyright © 2008 by The Templar Company plc

1 3 5 7 9 10 8 6 4 2

All rights reserved

ISBN 978-1-84011-353-2

Illustrations and design by Jonathan Lambert

Text by A. J. Wood

Manufactured in China

snuffle
and the egg

Limerick
County Library
00649492

jonathan lambert • a.j. wood

Limerick County Library

Say hello to Snuffle.

Snuffle is looking for someone to play with.

STOMP   STOMP   STOMP

He snuffles along and finds something
lying on the ground.

It is yellow. It is smooth, and it rolls!

What can it be?

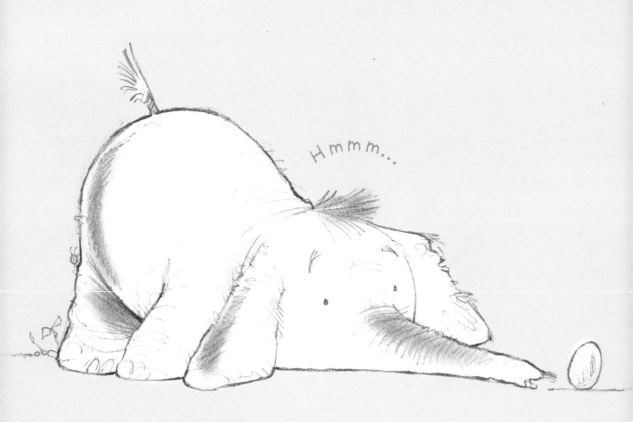

It is an egg. Perhaps he can play with it?

Then Snuffle remembers
that eggs break very easily.

Snuffle picks up the egg very carefully.

Ummm!

He tries moving it around.

He balances it on the end of his trunk...

He blows it gently up in the air.

Holding it with his trunk,
he runs this way…

and that way!

The egg does not break.

But then – *whoops!* –

Snuffle trips over!

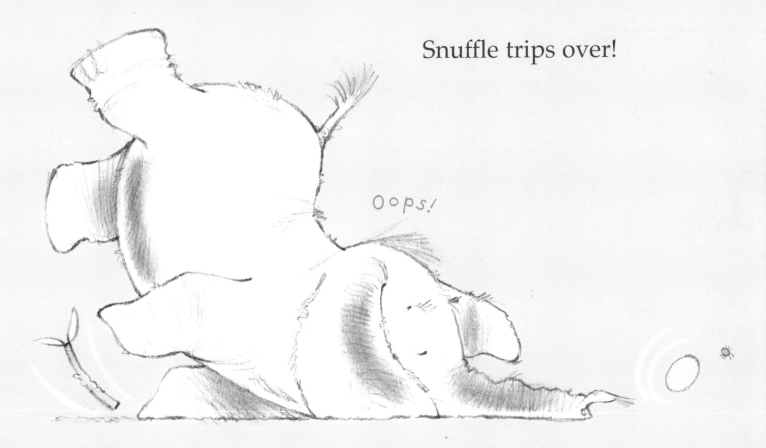

The egg lands with a *crack!*

Oh dear!

Snuffle runs away.

crack

The egg is *broken!*

Just then, Snuffle hears a different noise.

What could it be?

Snuffle watches…

Crack! Crack!

A little head pokes out!

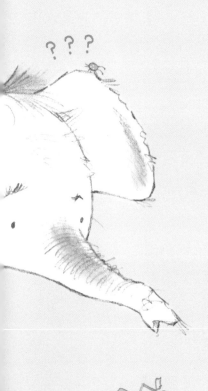

It is a *bird!*

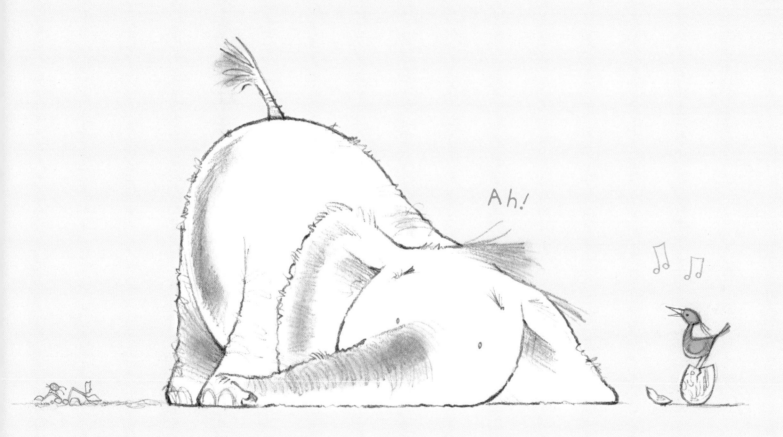

The bird flies into the air.

Oooo!

Snuffle is amazed!

The bird flies around Snuffle.

Snuffle likes the bird.

The bird plays with Snuffle.

Snuffle chases the bird.

When the bird flies away...
Snuffle is sad.

Oh!

But when the bird flies back...
Snuffle is happy again!

With him, the bird brings friends…

more and more friends!

But Snuffle is *very* happy,
because you can never have too many friends…
or can you?

Limerick County Library

00649 492

The end